# ABCs
## at the Haunted House

by Jennifer Marino Walters

illustrated by Nathan Y. Jarvis

RED
CHAIR
•PRESS•

Ghosts and goblins, monsters and mice.
What will we discover from A to Z in the
Halloween Haunted House?

Let's go for **apples**!

**BOO**—it's a bat! How about that!

**Candy corn**—yum!

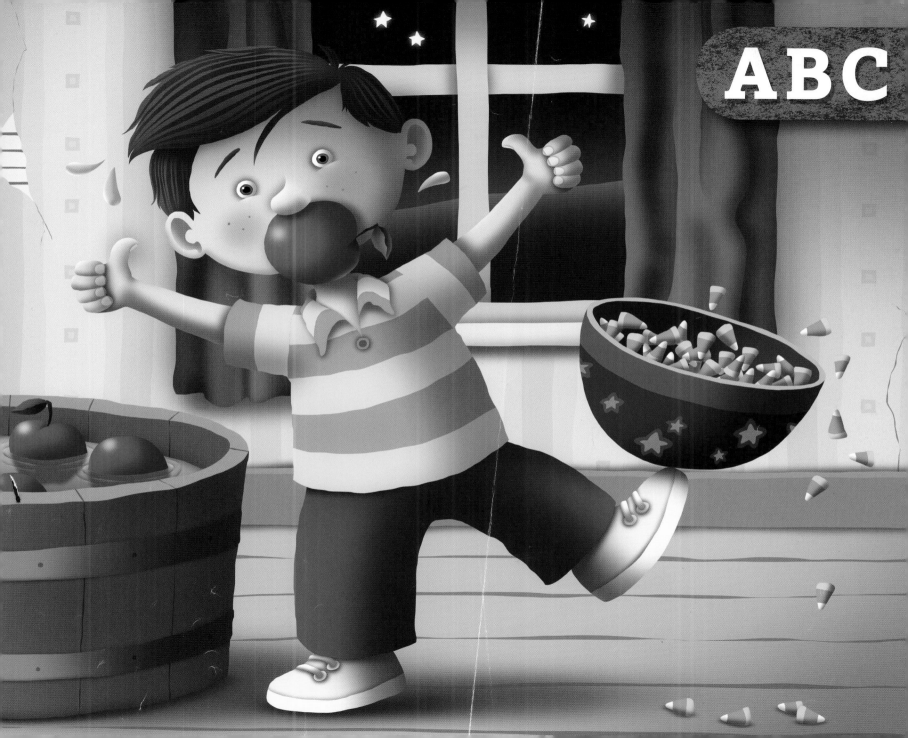

This house is full of **dark** places...
...**Eyes** spying on you and me!

**Freaky fangs** all around.

A **Giggly ghost** is our guide.

**Headstones** make for a **Happy Halloween**!

Our **invitation** welcomes us to a spooky good time!

Jack o' lanterns are a **jolly** idea.

A **Kitty** in black leaps by a **lantern**.

Look now! Is that a **mommy** or a **mummy**?

**Nighttime** can be fun at a haunted house.

An **Owl** watches all the action—hoot, hoot!

**Pumpkins** come in all sizes.

**Quivering** bones...

...little brown **rats**

**Spooky spiderwebs** complete the scene!

**Trick or treat!**

What's **under** the stairs? Be careful!

Two more spooky friends are on their way to our haunted party.

Make way for **Vampire** and the **Witch**!

Have you seen a skeleton in an **X-ray**?
Be eXtra careful!

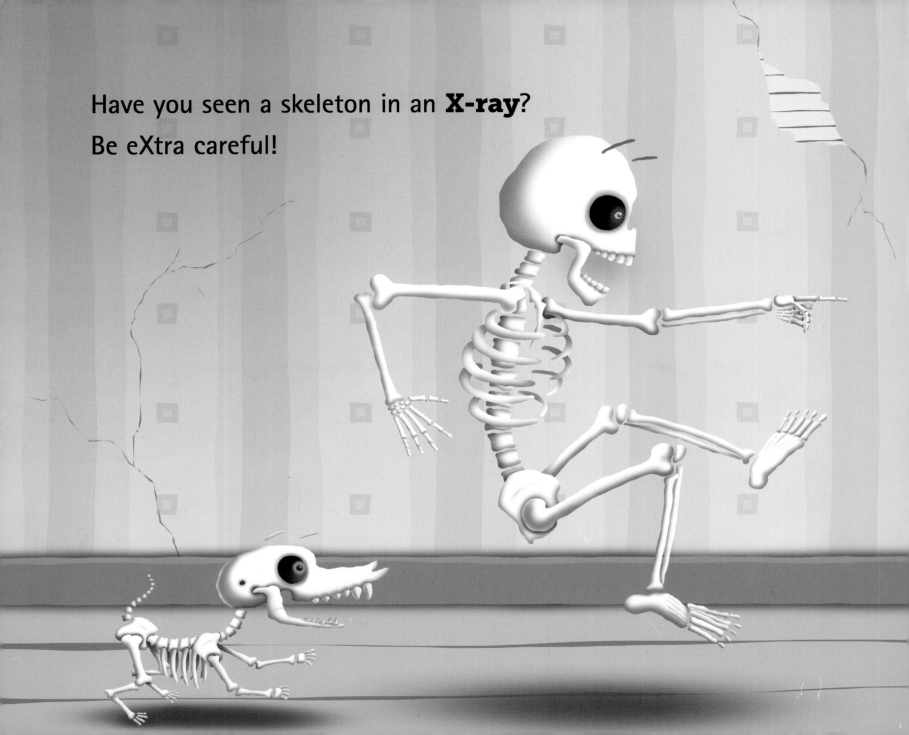

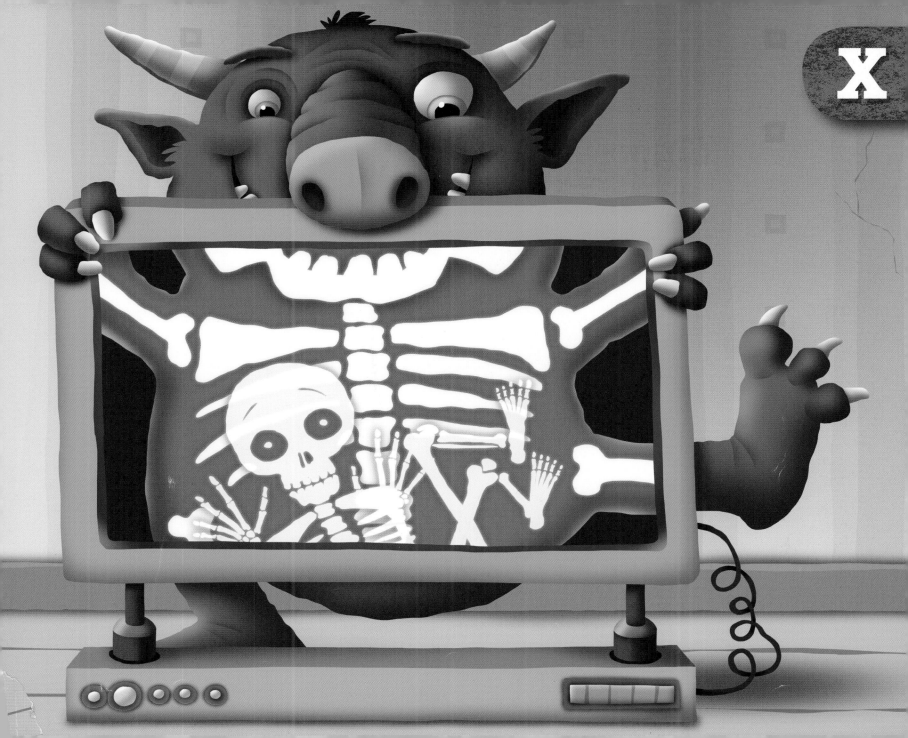

**Yikes!** A silly skeleton is not as scary as a **zombie**!

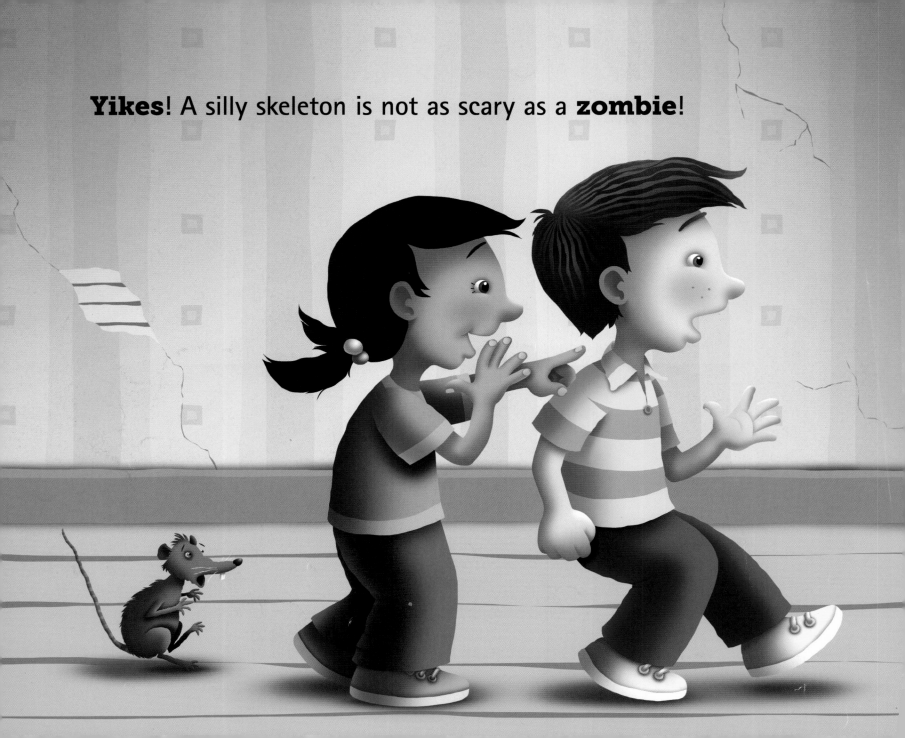

# This house is haunted from A to Z.

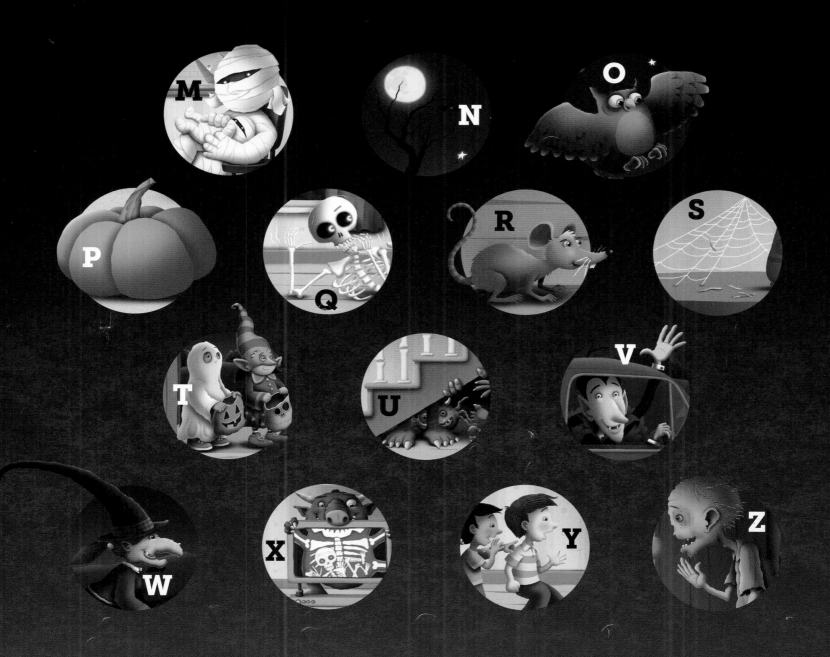

**Publisher's Cataloging-In-Publication Data**

Names: Marino Walters, Jennifer, author. | Jarvis, Nathan Y.,
    illustrator.

Title: ABCs at the haunted house / by Jennifer Marino Walters ;
    illustrated by Nathan Y. Jarvis.

Description: [South Egremont, Massachusetts] : Red Chair Press,
    [2019] | Interest age level: 004-008. | Summary: "A lively
    illustrated walk through a spooky fun Halloween Haunted House
    to discover the alphabet along the way."--Provided by publisher.

Identifiers: ISBN 9781634408769 (hardcover) | ISBN 9781634408776
    (ebook)

Subjects: LCSH: Haunted houses--Juvenile fiction. | English
    language--Alphabet--Juvenile fiction. | CYAC: Haunted houses--
    Fiction. | English language--Alphabet--Fiction. | LCGFT:
    Alphabet books.

Classification: LCC PZ7.1.W358 Ab 2019 (print) | LCC PZ7.1.W358
    (ebook) | DDC [E]--dc23

LCCN: 2018962622

Printed in the United States of America

0519 1P CGF19